MEDICI BOOKS FOR CHILDREN

Jiggy's Treasure Hunt
by Molly Brett

© The Medici Society Ltd., London 1973
Printed in England · Code 85503028 3

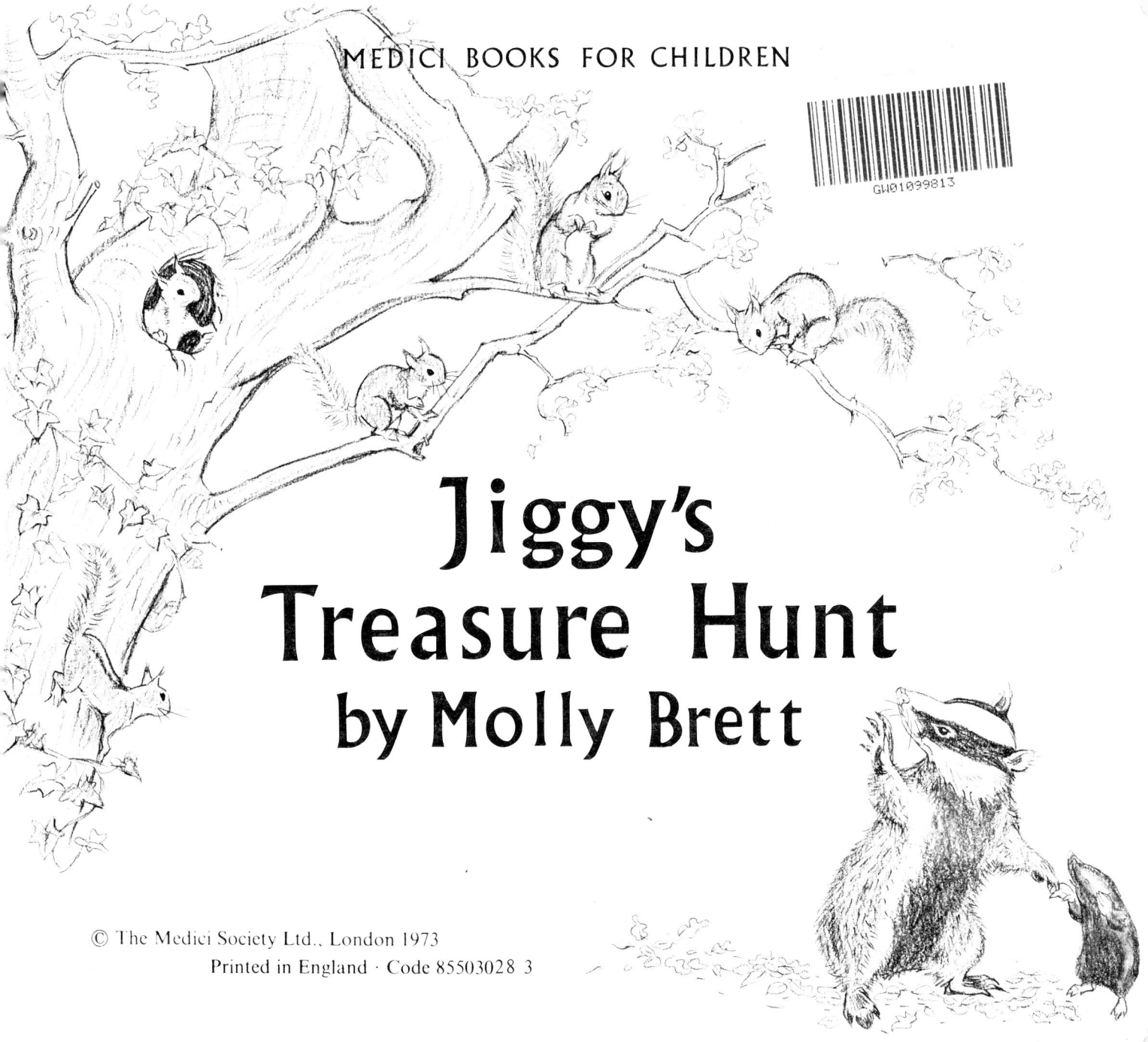

"Never knew nuts to be so scarce—and not one to store for the winter!" chattered Jiggy the red squirrel as she searched busily among the fallen leaves and scratched into the soil beneath, and then suddenly—JIGGY DISAPPEARED! There was only a big black hole to be seen as she fell into a dark passage below.

Peeping round a corner she saw a little figure digging by the light of two glow worms. It was Mr. Mouldiwarp the mole and he was very surprised to see her.

"A tree top animal in my tunnel!" he grunted, "how did *you* get here?"

"I fell in," explained Jiggy, "and now—where do I get out?"

The mole looked doubtful, "My passage is very small in places and it will be a tight squeeze with that big tail of yours," he told her.

So he started to enlarge the sides of the tunnel, but there seemed to be a big stone wedged among the tree roots which got in the way.

Mr. Mouldiwarp scratched and scraped and at last—out came an old earthenware pot which broke as it fell to the ground, and among the pieces was a piece of silver birch bark. The mole was too short-sighted to see the faded writing on it and handed it to Jiggy who read out:—

THE HIDDEN TREASURE OF GRANDPA GINGERNUT.
"If my Treasure you will take,
Cross the fields and swim the lake,
Then—take care you are not seen,
Run across the village green,
Along a lane and in a mile
Hop over gate and then a stile.
Climb the hill and you will see
On its top a great big tree,
Dig round about and you shall find
Nuts, NUTS, NUTS of every kind."

The little squirrel jumped up and down in excitement for she had often heard of her great—many great—grandfather's treasure hoard.

"I must find it at once!" she squeaked, "and then—no more hunting for a winter store of nuts."

So Mr. Mouldiwarp led her to his front door; pointing with a pink paw to a line of mole hills he grunted, "Follow those and you will come to the lake."

Skipping along the tops of trees and stone walls Jiggy soon came to the water's edge, but it was much too wide and deep to swim across. Then the squirrel saw an old bird's nest nearby, strongly made, lined with dried mud, from which the birds had flown away long ago. It floated beautifully and, hoisting a large leaf for a sail, Jiggy pushed off.

But soon the nest began to rock and looking into the water she saw a big fierce pike fish and—he was trying to upset her boat!

"Help! help!" squeaked the squirrel as the nest tilted over and then, just as the pike opened his jaws to seize her, there was a rush of strong wings overhead and Longbeak the heron pounced down on the fish, who quickly disappeared into the depths below.

So Jiggy sailed on safely until her boat grounded gently on the opposite shore, where she climbed a tree and looking down saw cottages clustered round a green, and on it the Village Fête was set out.

The stallholders were at lunch and all was quiet, so the inquisitive Jiggy hopped on to the tables piled with fruit, flowers, knitting, needlework, and many other things.

There was a tempting basket of walnuts on one stall but, as Jiggy tried to take one, she upset a pile of apples which rolled away in all directions. Then she heard footsteps coming, scrambled under a tent and hid in a big umbrella just inside.

Soon the Fête was ready to begin; an important lady in a large hat was to open it. But as she began her speech it started to rain and the umbrella was hastily raised over the lady and her hat.

Down bounced Jiggy on top of the hat much to everyone's surprise.

"There's a Cat on my Hat!" exclaimed the lady in some agitation and the boy scouts in charge of the balloons rushed forward to help. In the excitement the balloons broke loose, and away they floated as Jiggy skipped up a tree, while the important lady was comforted, the rain stopped, the balloons were collected, and cups of tea appeared in the biggest tent.

But the little squirrel remained hidden among the leaves until the fête was over and all was quiet once more on the village green.

Then in the twilight she ran quickly across it repeating:—

"Down the lane and in a mile,
Hop over gate and then a stile."

But instead of a lane there was a busy road with traffic streaming along it to bar the way. So Jiggy ran along the roadside until the trees arched over and she was able to leap with airy grace from branch to branch, finally crossing safely with one big jump.

She found a gate and inside was a car park, so the squirrel crept through a jungle of wheels and reached the stile beyond. As it was now dark she curled up in some bushes and slept until morning.

Jiggy woke early and remembering:—

"Climb the hill and you will see
On its top a great big tree."

She looked—and looked for—there in the dawn light was *the hill*—but it was *covered* with big trees and under which of them could the treasure be buried?

As the little squirrel stared, puzzled and disappointed, a large paw patted her on the shoulder, and she looked up into the striped face of Mr. Bruff the badger.

So Jiggy told him of her treasure hunt, "Instead of *one* tree there are so many that I shall *never* find the right one," she sniffed.

The badger started to laugh, "There's your treasure right before your eyes," he chuckled, "your grandpa Gingernut buried his nuts in the ground, they sent out roots and shoots, and grew after many a year into these big trees, all bearing nuts which are yours for the taking."

In a moment Jiggy skipped up the hill among the trees, and there indeed was her treasure. Hazel nuts grew in bunches, tall chestnuts dropped prickly husks with fat nuts inside, beechnuts covered the ground, and shining acorns hung on the oaks.

"Thank you! Thank you!" she chattered to the badger, "I am the richest red squirrel in the world!"

In the bright autumn days that followed Jiggy gathered nuts for the winter and stored them in a hollow tree but—the nuts disappeared!

Then she found a tail sticking out of her store cupboard; Grizzle and Guzzle the grey squirrels were helping themselves.

"We are very hungry," they squeaked, so the kindhearted Jiggy invited them to tea, but after that they came for breakfast, dinner, tea, and supper, and grew fatter and fatter, while Jiggy had to work hard to replenish her larder, for winter was now very near.

Before the animals in the wood went to sleep during the cold dark days she asked them all to a party in honour of her friend the badger, but the two greedy grey squirrels were not invited. "They would gobble up everything," said Jiggy.

So the invitation cards were written out with blackberry juice on bright yellow autumn leaves, and on the day of the party all the animals in the wood gathered to enjoy the games and good things to eat.

Grizzle and Guzzle were very cross about not being asked to the party and started to throw fir cones at Jiggy and her guests, but Mr. Bruff soon picked up those two bad little squirrels and threw them out of the wood.

Away they rolled down the hillside ending up in a patch of nettles, where they plotted revenge with Robber Rat from the farm barn who had also been left out of the party.

"We will capture Jiggy and throw her into the lake, then the wood and all her nuts will be ours," they chuckled.

All three were very frightened of her friend the big badger until Guzzle pointed out, "He *sleeps* most of the day and only goes round the wood at night."

But they forgot to *whisper* and a pair of long ears heard their plan so Mr. Bruff and Jiggy soon heard the news from a small rabbit.

The little squirrel was frightened but the badger grunted, "I'll give Grizzle and Guzzle such a surprise that they will never come near your wood again." Then he went off chuckling as snowflakes drifted down through the branches to show that winter had come at last.

Next morning the grey squirrels and Robber Rat started up the snow covered hillside to capture Jiggy. Suddenly Robber Rat stopped, "Didn't you say there was just *one* badger in the wood?" he demanded. "But *I* see hundreds of badger tracks in the snow!"

Guzzle stared at the footprints and they were all leading *into* the wood.

"Then there must be *hundreds* of badgers in there!" squeaked Grizzle, "and—not *one* of them has come out again—Mr. Bruff must be living here now with his brothers, sisters, cousins, uncles and aunts!"

Robber Rat turned tail and scuttled off, followed by those two naughty squirrels, for none of them dare face all those badgers—and they never came back.

Then from behind a tree peered the striped face of—just one badger, and down from a branch skipped Jiggy.

"How did you do it?" she questioned, "and why have they all run away?"

Mr. Bruff laughed and laughed, "Maybe *you* don't know, and certainly Guzzle and his friends don't know that Badger can run *backwards* as well as forwards," he chuckled. "In and out, to and fro, and round about, I went last night, but all my footprints in the snow pointed *into* the wood and not one came *out* again, so it looked as if the wood was full of badgers."

Then Jiggy stayed safely in the wood her great—many greats—grandpa Gingernut had planted, with plenty of nuts in store for the winter she slept away the cold dark days in a cosy nest, with her beautiful tail curled round her.

In the spring Mr. Bruff found a smart young red squirrel whose tail had been run over by a car, so Jiggy cared for him until he was well again.

Soon the two were chasing each other round the tree trunks, swinging on the topmost branches, feasting on nuts, and had a fine house high up in a hollow tree.

Now there are red squirrels in Great Grandpa Gingernut's wood again, and Mr. Bruff the badger tells the tale of the treasure hunt when he is asked to babysit with Jiggy's three babies who are called Hazel, Conker, and Cobnut.